Paradise Sleep™
Presents:

The MAGIC Ice Cream Palace

By: Jose Colon M.D.,MPH

Illustrated by: Amy Rottinger

Halo ●●●●
Publishing International

ISBN 13: 978-1-61244-260-0
Library of Congress Control Number: 2014903358

Printed in the United States of America

www.halopublishing.com

Published by Halo Publishing International
AP·726
P.O. Box 60326
Houston, Texas 77205
Toll Free 1-877-705-9647
www.halopublishing.com
www.holapublishing.com
e-mail: contact@halopublishing.com

I dedicate this book to my two biggest fans, Manuel and Jada-Love. I look forward to reading you a story every night. I enjoy picking you up from school around story time so I can read to your class as well. Mommy and Daddy love you.

I wish an equal dedication to the families who help make this a creative world for our family.

Encourage others to encourage others.
—Jose Colon, M.D., MPH

"*The Magic Ice Cream Palace* is a lovely introduction to relaxation and self-regulation for young children that focuses on the transition to sleep. This transition is often challenging for both children and parents, so this gentle tale of a little boy and his vivid imagination will be a welcome addition to the bedtime story library. It's a rare child who doesn't like ice cream and a rare parent who won't enjoy sharing this story with their little sleepy head."

—Judith Owens M.D., MPH. Director of Sleep Medicine, Children's National Medical Center. Pediatrics, George Washington University.

Author of multiple pediatric sleep books including *Take Charge of Your Child's Sleep: The All-in-One Resource for Solving Sleep Problems in Kids and Teens.*

Once upon a time—the time is now—a young boy named Wawa decides to use his wonderful imagination to visit the Magic Ice Cream Palace.

Wawa walks up hills to get there. However, the hills are not made of grass. They are scoops of vanilla ice cream. He feels the cold softness on his feet.

4

Wawa sees a river of melted chocolate, and wishes his feet were warm.

Help Wawa out. Close your eyes. Take a calming in-breath through your nose.

Bring all your attention to your feet and breathe out slowly.

Wawa hears the sound of cool air pass through his nose. He feels the air turn warm and silky as he breaths out slooowly. He looks down and sees warm chocolate boots. He feels a calming sensation on his feet.

As he walks, he leaves chocolate footprints on the ice cream hills. A cold wind blows and hardens the chocolate footprints.

This is how they make chocolate-chip ice cream in the Magic Ice Cream Palace.

The cold wind makes Wawa's legs and knees shiver.

Help Wawa out. Close your eyes. Take a relaxing in-breath through your nose.

Bring all your attention to your legs and breathe out slowly.

Bring all your attention to your knees and breathe out slowly.

Wawa thinks of his favorite color, which is green. He opens his eyes and looks down. He is wearing green snow pants. He feels a calming sensation in his legs.

As he walks around with his green snow pants, the ice cream turns green.

This is how they make mint chocolate-chip ice cream in the Magic Ice Cream Palace.

Wawa reaches the hilltop and looks down. He sees a slope.
Thinking it would be fun to slide down the hill, he sits down.
Wawa realizes his hips and tushie are cold!

Help Wawa out. Close your eyes. Take a peaceful in-breath through your nose.

Bring all your attention to your hips and breathe out slowly.

Bring all your attention to your seat and breathe out slowly.

Wawa finds himself sitting on a banana sled. He feels a calming sensation in his lower body.

He glides down the slope. He swerves left and picks strawberries. He sees a big walnut tree and swerves right to avoid it.

Wawa crashes into the tree. The banana sled splits in half. The strawberries seep into the ice cream. The tree falls over and splashes into the chocolate river. Chocolate splashes all over the ice cream. The walnuts break to pieces and scatter everywhere.

This is how they make banana split sundaes in the Magic Ice Cream Palace.

Wawa hears Violet and her brother Bam playing and laughing. They are throwing snowballs made of ice cream. "Come play with us," Violet calls to Wawa.

"My sister likes to play and loves ice cream! Can I imagine she is with me?" asks Wawa.

"This is a creative world. You can imagine anything you want!" replies Miss Barbara, the baker as she is taking fresh cakes from the oven.

Wawa's sister, Baby Love, appears. She likes to catch snowflakes made of sprinkles with her tongue.

17

Wawa reaches down to make an ice cream snowball. However, his hands are cold.

Help Wawa out. Close your eyes. Take a mind clearing in-breath through your nose.

Bring all your awareness to the palms of your hands and breathe out slowly.

Bring all your awareness to your thumbs and breathe out slowly.

Bring all your awareness to your fingertips and breathe out slowly.

Wawa sees warm gloves on his hands. He feels a calming sensation in his hands.

Wawa joins the ice cream snowball fun. He smells freshly baked cakes and sees them cooling on the windowsill of Miss Barbara's Bakery. Ice cream powder dusts them all over.

This is how they make ice cream cake in the Magic Ice Cream Palace.

Wawa sees it is getting dark. His body is warm, but his neck and head feel cold.

Help Wawa out. Close your eyes. Take a sleepy in-breath through your nose.

Bring all your awareness to your shoulders and breathe out slowly.

Bring all your awareness to your neck and breathe out slowly.

Bring all your awareness to your head and breathe out slowly.

Wawa is now wearing a warm waffle-cone scarf and hat. He feels a calming sensation all around his head, and his mind feels clear and happy. He yawns.

All the children feel calm and happy. They follow WASO the owl as they walk through the hall of magic bedroom doors. The children find a door that matches their own.

Wawa opens Baby Love's door for her.

Wawa finds his door and is magically in his room. He is wearing his pajamas. He still feels the calming sensation of his boots, snow pants, gloves and headgear. While in bed, he even does another body scan, bringing his focused attention to his feet all the way up his body. Before he is finished, he scans one more part of his body—his heart.

He smiles softly. He feels a calming sensation in his heart and mind.

Once upon a time—the time is now—when you close your eyes and rest your head on a soft pillow, the story becomes your own.

How to Use Paradise Sleep Children's Books

First and foremost, enjoy the book with your kids. That's why instructions are at the end!

Paradise Sleep Children's Books help teach children self-regulation skills through story and metaphor. There is also an emphasis in living in the present moment. The Magic Ice Cream Palace teaches body scan, an exercise that evokes a relaxation response.

Sleep Hygiene

Bedtime can be difficult for parents and children, but it doesn't have to be. Bedtime has the opportunity to be a bonding experience for children and parents. Using going to bed early as a punishment may lead to sleep-avoiding behavior. Emphasizing bedtime as story time builds a positive experience your child may look forward to and remember life long.

Encourage Creativity

Encourage the development of the child's wonderful imagination. There may be features of an illustration a child may want to expand upon. As parents, guide this with statements such as "Hmmm, I wonder what kind of ice cream that is?" as you point to the ice cream scoop with the palm tree and coconut.

Note: Asking too many questions during a story may take the child out of the dream-like state and they may become tangential.

Sleep-Avoiding Behavior

Just before going to bed, the mind is often receptive to thoughts and ideas. As adults, if we have work or stress related thoughts prior to bed, we have a tendency to repeat these words in our head. This is evident when an adult states their mind has "racing thoughts" while in bed. Racing thoughts in a child may lead to sleep-avoiding behavior. This is evident in children when they come out and ask for water, hugs or express, "I need to tell you something." Stories help calm the mind.

Emphasizing the silly fun of a story before bed helps reduce the initial sleep-avoiding behavior of getting into bed.

Calming the Mind

The left hemisphere of your brain is your language area; it is logical and likes words. It can be a source of racing thoughts. The right hemisphere of your brain is creative and imaginative. When you stimulate the right brain with imagination, the verbal centers of the left brain are effectively shushed.

Children and adults alike have racing thoughts; children, however, are still developing their self-regulation skills for impulse control. A child may see a new toy and run to it, then see a friend and leave the toy, feel an itch in their nose and pick it, and so forth as they run amok. Commonly with the mention of story time, a child comes to a wide-eyed halt as the creative world of the right brain shushes the left brain. Encouraging them to use their wonderful imagination with their eyes closed may help calm the racing mind.

Relaxation Response

Body scan is a method used to help control the racing mind. This technique has been found useful for improving sleep, decreasing stress and improving comfort (decreasing pain). In body scan, beginning with a particular body part, one would focus on soothing sensations. Each body part is relaxed for approximately less than a minute.

By practicing this with children, the child also is practicing skills of focused attention. Over time, as the child's focused attention skills are cultivated, they will be able to scan each body part a little longer and learn to form a relaxation response for self-regulation.

Follow Your Breath

Once or twice within the book, as your child helps Wawa out, ask them about their breathing. Is your breath cool when you breathe in?
Is your breath warm and silky when you breathe out?

Emphasize to the child to breathe out slowly to help Wawa get more of the warm feelings. People often say, "Take a deep breath" to calm down. However, a better way to visualize this is to "Breath out slowly." It's the exhalation that calms the body and mind.

Yogic breathing and mindfulness practice emphasize longer exhalations and shorter natural inhalations. Ask the child to listen to the sound of the air passing back and forth through his or her airway; ask them to "Follow your breath." This evokes a relaxation response and cultivates self-regulation. You may also have them imitate the cold wind by softly blowing on the pages to allow the pages to turn.

Note: When you see them yawning, you taught them just right!

The Present Moment

Paradise Sleep Children's Books emphasize living in the present moment, which is why they are written in the present tense. This also empowers the child to continue the story in their mind once their eyes close. When a child embraces their wonderful imagination and can exercise self-regulation skills, this may help reduce disruptive behavior in the daytime as well as reduce sleep-avoiding behavior at night.

Social Skills

In everyday life when you see the child experiencing a moment similar to the story in the book, remind them about how a character reacted in the story. For example, Wawa opens the door for his sister. Compliment your kids when they hold the door open for others, just like Wawa in the book.

Mirroring

When a parent practices a form of relaxation therapy, a child may mirror this themselves. Kids often mirror parental habits. Even a toddler with a one-word phrase vocabulary may pick up a toy phone, tilt their head and say, "Hello?" as they've seen their parent do this. Parents are encouraged to develop their own relaxation responses, whether it is through mindfulness, yoga, self-hypnosis or meditation.

Follow the adventures of WASO the owl at *www.ParadiseSleep.com*.

CPSIA information can be obtained
at www.ICGtesting.com
Printed in the USA
BVXC01n1624190314
348113BV00004B/63

9 781612 442600